Note to the Reader

Gender equality is crucial to a just, fair and respectful society and c[...] to children from an early age. In my experience as both a mother a[...] difference between the genders until competition starts to seep into their lives. Once this begins, roles between the sexes become more defined. Sadly, many young girls begin to feel less empowered and often take a 'back seat' to their male peers. My aim in writing this book is to empower young girls to take a 'front seat' and to have an active leadership role in society, and for boys to see that there is no difference between the genders in terms of abilities. Respect for one another regardless of gender or race is key. We are a diverse society and all who participate in it have skills and gifts to offer — gender or race is irrelevant. For children to learn this from a young age is empowering. Captain Pearl Fairweather is a just and fair leader. And yes, in society we do need leaders, but we need leaders who show respect for the opinions of others and lead with grace and compassion. In summary, my key aim in writing this book is to empower young girls and for boys to respect that empowerment, and to embrace and value it. Boys' lives can be so much richer if they partner with girls on an even footing with each individual contributing their talents unreservedly. On pages 36–38 you will find Discussion Questions to assist in drawing out the learning.

As a little girl growing up on a dairy farm, I would often stand in an **old bathtub,** hoist a flag and imagine that I was **sailing the seven seas** in search of **adventure.** At the age of **21** I did just that! J.S.

PEARL FAIRWEATHER

Pirate Captain

by Jayneen Sanders
illustrated by Lesley Danson

Teaching children about gender equality, respect,
respectful relationships, empowerment, diversity, leadership,
recognizing bullying behaviours, and the prevention of violence

Dedication

To my wonderful husband, Mark,
because from the moment we met,
equality was always a given.
Love you so much. J.S.

For Mum. L.D.

Pearl Fairweather, Pirate Captain
Educate2Empower Publishing an imprint of
UpLoad Publishing Pty Ltd
Victoria Australia
www.upload.com.au

First published in 2016

Text copyright © Jayneen Sanders 2016
Illustration copyright © Lesley Danson 2016

Written by Jayneen Sanders
Illustrations by Lesley Danson

Designed by Susannah Low, Butterflyrocket Design

Printed in China through Book Production Solutions

Cataloguing-in-Publication Data
National Library of Australia

Creator:	Sanders, Jayneen, author.
Title:	Pearl Fairweather, Pirate Captain : teaching children about gender equality, respect, respectful relationships, empowerment, diversity, leadership, recognizing bullying behaviors, and the prevention of violence / Jayneen Sanders ; Lesley Danson, illustrator.
ISBN:	9781925089257 (paperback)
Subjects:	Pirates--Juvenile fiction. Individual differences--Juvenile fiction. Respect for persons--Juvenile fiction. Interpersonal relations--Juvenile fiction. Leadership in children--Juvenile fiction. Bullying--Prevention--Juvenile fiction.
Other Creators/Contributors:	Danson, Lesley, illustrator.
Dewey Number:	A823.4

About the Author

Jayneen Sanders (aka Jay Dale) is an experienced classroom teacher, the lead author for 'Engage Literacy' (published by Capstone Classroom in the US) and has authored over 100 books for children, a publisher of educational materials, and the mother of three children. She is also the proud author of the children's book on safe and unsafe touch, 'Some Secrets Should Never Be Kept' and the parents' guide 'Body Safety Education — A parents' guide to protecting kids from sexual abuse'. Jayneen is a passionate advocate for Body Safety Education to be taught in homes and schools. She has written teaching notes to support her resources, empowering books for children such as 'No Means No!' and numerous blogs and articles on teaching Body Safety.

For more information on Jayneen's books and related topics go to:

e2epublishing.info

Books by the Same Author

Some Secrets Should Never Be Kept

'Some Secrets Should Never Be Kept' is an award-winning and beautifully illustrated children's book that sensitively broaches the subject of inappropriate touch. This book was written as a tool to help parents, caregivers and teachers broach the subject with children in an age-appropriate and non-threatening way. 'Some Secrets Should Never Be Kept' is now integrated into Body Safety programs throughout the United States, the United Kingdom and Australasia. It has been translated into seven languages and is published by Memory House in China. Suitable for children 3 to 11 years.

Body Safety Education
A parents' guide to protecting kids from sexual abuse

This essential and easy-to-read guide contains simple, practical and age-appropriate ideas on how parents and carers can protect children from sexual abuse — ensuring they grow up as assertive and confident teenagers and adults. It is crucial we empower our children through education. There is no downside to teaching children Body Safety!

No Means No!
Teaching children about personal boundaries, respect and consent; empowering kids by respecting their choices and their right to say, 'No!'

'No Means No!' is a children's picture book about an empowered little girl who has a very strong and clear voice in all issues, especially those relating to her body and personal boundaries. This book can be read to children from 2 to 9 years. It is a springboard for discussions regarding children's choices and their rights. The 'Note to the Reader' at the beginning of the book and the 'Discussion Questions' on the final pages guide and enhance this essential discussion.

Even though Captain McCross was in a small boat far below Pearl's big ship, he was **still** being rude. Why do you think he acted like that? Why didn't Captain McCross just simply ask for help in a nice manner? If he had asked for help in a kind manner, do you think Pearl would have helped Captain McCross and his crew? Why do you say that? Do you think Pearl should let him come aboard? Why? Why not? What would you have done if you were Captain Pearl Fairweather?

Pages 22-23

What does 'conditions' mean? Do you think Pearl's conditions were fair? Why do you say that? Should people try to work together in harmony and show respect for one another? Why? Why not? Do you think we should respect one another in this classroom/house? Why do you say that? How might we do better? Was Pearl right to tell Captain McCross she did not want him to take over her ship? Why do you say that? Can people take things away from other people just because they want to? Why? Why not? Why do you think Captain McCross would not agree to these conditions (rules)? Would you agree to these conditions? Why? Why not?

Pages 24-25

Was Pearl right to ask the crew of the *Scurvy Dog* what they wished to do? Why do you say that? Why do you think the crew was happy to agree to Pearl's conditions? Do you think they will be happy working with all the other pirates on *Harmony*? Why do you say that? Would you be happy working on Pearl's ship? Why? Why not?

Pages 26-27

Why did Captain Pearl say to Captain McCross, 'Then that is your choice'? Sometimes we have choices. We can choose to work together or not. Do you think Captain McCross made the right decision? Why do you think that? Do you have choices in your life? What choices do you have? What is an 'angry pout'? Can you show me an angry pout?

Pages 28-29

Why did Pearl get the crew from the *Scurvy Dog* to sign a document with all the conditions listed? Do you think the crew will keep to these conditions? Why? Why not? Can people from many different countries work together in harmony? Why? Why not? Do you think the crew would need some rules that they would have to keep to? What rules do we have in this classroom/house? Why do we have these rules? Why did Captain McCross end up all alone in a small boat? Do you think he will ever change his ways? Why? Why not? Do we all need to change our ways from time to time? How might we have to change our ways?

Pages 30-31

What does 'worked together as one' mean? Why do you think two such different crews were able to work together? What qualities do people need to be able to work together successfully?

Pages 32-33

What do **you** think became of Captain Sandy McCross? Do you think he was happy? Why? Why not? Do you think he ever learned to change his ways? Why? Why not?

Page 34

What does it mean when the author says, 'Pearl and her crew continue to live their lives as they have always wanted'? Can we always live our lives as we want to? Do we have choices?

Why was Captain Pearl Fairweather a good and fair leader? What qualities did she have? What qualities do you have? Could you be a good and fair leader? I am sure you are a strong and fair leader and could do anything!

On the back cover, Captain Pearl Fairweather is described as 'brave'. Do you think, after reading this story, she is brave? Why do you say that? Do you think Captain McCross was a bully? Why do you say that? What do you think a bully is? How should we stand up to people who try to bully us?

place? What did he mean when he said, 'I want none of your useless crew'? Why didn't he want the crew? What would you have done if you had been Captain Pearl Fairweather? Should Captain McCross be speaking to Pearl in this manner? Why? Why not? Do you think Captain McCross is a bully? Why do you say that? Should Captain McCross call Pearl a 'silly goose'? Why not? Why is it rude to call people names? How does it make people feel when they are called names? Should we call people names when we don't get what we want? Can you explain what you mean? Captain McCross was being 'disrespectful'. What does this mean? What should you do if someone is being disrespectful?

Pages 12-13

Why do you think Captain Pearl Fairweather did not answer Captain McCross? Why did she simply turn away? What would you do if someone was shouting at you? What does 'calmly and with grace' mean? Why was Pearl so calm? Did Pearl do the right thing by turning her ship away or should she have stayed to fight? Do you think Pearl showed she was good leader? Why do you say that?

What does 'not on your nelly?' mean? (Definition: Cockney rhyming slang for 'not on your life'. Nelly rhymes with smelly, which moves on to smelly breath, breath moves on to breathing to keep alive, which then leads to 'not on your life'.) Do you think Pearl was right to stand up to Captain McCross? Why do you say that? Why did Captain McCross decide to 'weather the storm' in the seas around the Islands of Plenty? Why has the author described him as 'rather silly'? What does 'tranquillity' mean? Why do you think Pearl and her crew sailed *Harmony* to the Bay of Tranquillity? What do you think is going to happen to Captain McCross and the crew on the *Scurvy Dog*? Do you think it was kind of Pearl to warn Captain McCross about the storm? Why? Why not? Why does Captain McCross think that he knows better than Captain Pearl Fairweather? Does Captain McCross think he is more powerful than Pearl? Why might he think that?

Pages 16-17

What do you think 'tucked away' means? Do you think *Harmony* is safe tucked away in the Bay of Tranquillity? Why? Why not? What do you think might be happening to the *Scurvy Dog* and her crew in the open sea?

Pages 18-19

Oh dear! What has happened here? Do you think Captain McCross wishes now he had listened to Captain Pearl Fairweather's advice? Why do you say that? Is it a good idea to always listen to people's advice? Why? Why not? Do you always have to do what other people say? Whose advice do you listen to? Why do you listen to that person? What things do you like about that person?

Pages 20-21

What do you think Pearl was really thinking when she saw the crew from the *Scurvy Dog* drifting towards her ship? When Pearl said, 'I suppose you want my ship?' was she being serious? Why do you say that?

Discussion Questions

for Parents, Caregivers and Educators

The following Discussion Questions are intended as a guide and can be used to initiate an open dialogue with your child. They are optional and/or can be explored at different readings as there are far too many questions to ask in one reading. I suggest you allow your child time to answer the questions and to ask some of their own. It is important that you value their input and listen to their voice. 'Pearl Fairweather, Pirate Captain' can be used as a teaching springboard for discussions around gender equality, respect, respectful relationships, empowerment, diversity, leadership, recognizing bullying behaviours, and the prevention of violence. All of these discussions only increase your child's sense of self-worth, their confidence and empowerment.

Pages 4-5

Do you think Pearl's mother and grandmother were pirates? What kind of pirates do you think they were? Why do you think Pearl was different from other pirates?

Pages 6-7

What kind of adventures might Pearl have had? Where might she sail too? Why do you think Pearl stood tall and proud at the bow of her ship? What do you think the author meant when she wrote, 'the sea had gifted calm'?

Pages 8-9

Why do you think sailors came from all over the world to join Captain Pearl Fairweather on the good ship *Harmony*? Do you think Pearl was good leader? Why do you say that? What qualities might a good leader have? Do you think people from different countries can live and work together peacefully? Why do you say that? Why do you think 'never a cross word was spoken' on Captain Pearl's ship? Why do you think Pearl's ship was called *Harmony*? What do you do if someone speaks to you in a cross or angry manner? Do you work well with: others in your classroom/ your brother/sister at home? Why do you say that? How might you/the students in your classroom work together in a more respectful way? Why do you think the author has written, 'one cloudy afternoon' when Captain McCross is introduced into the story? Can you guess what type of character Captain McCross will be?

Pages 10-11

Do you think Captain McCross was rude when he said, 'Give me your ship'? Did he have the right to take over Pearl's ship? Why? Why not? Why does he think he has the right to take over her ship? Why do you think he wanted to take over Pearl's ship in the first

And to this day, Captain Pearl Fairweather is well-loved and respected by her crew, and is known as a good, fair and strong captain. She and her crew continue to live their lives as they have always wanted — sailing the seven seas in search of adventure!

Pearl Fairweather was a pirate.

And just like her mother and grandmother before her, she was born to sail the seven seas in all their shades of blue and green.

Pearl was not like other pirates — she did not steal or harm. Pearl sailed the ocean blue looking only for adventure.

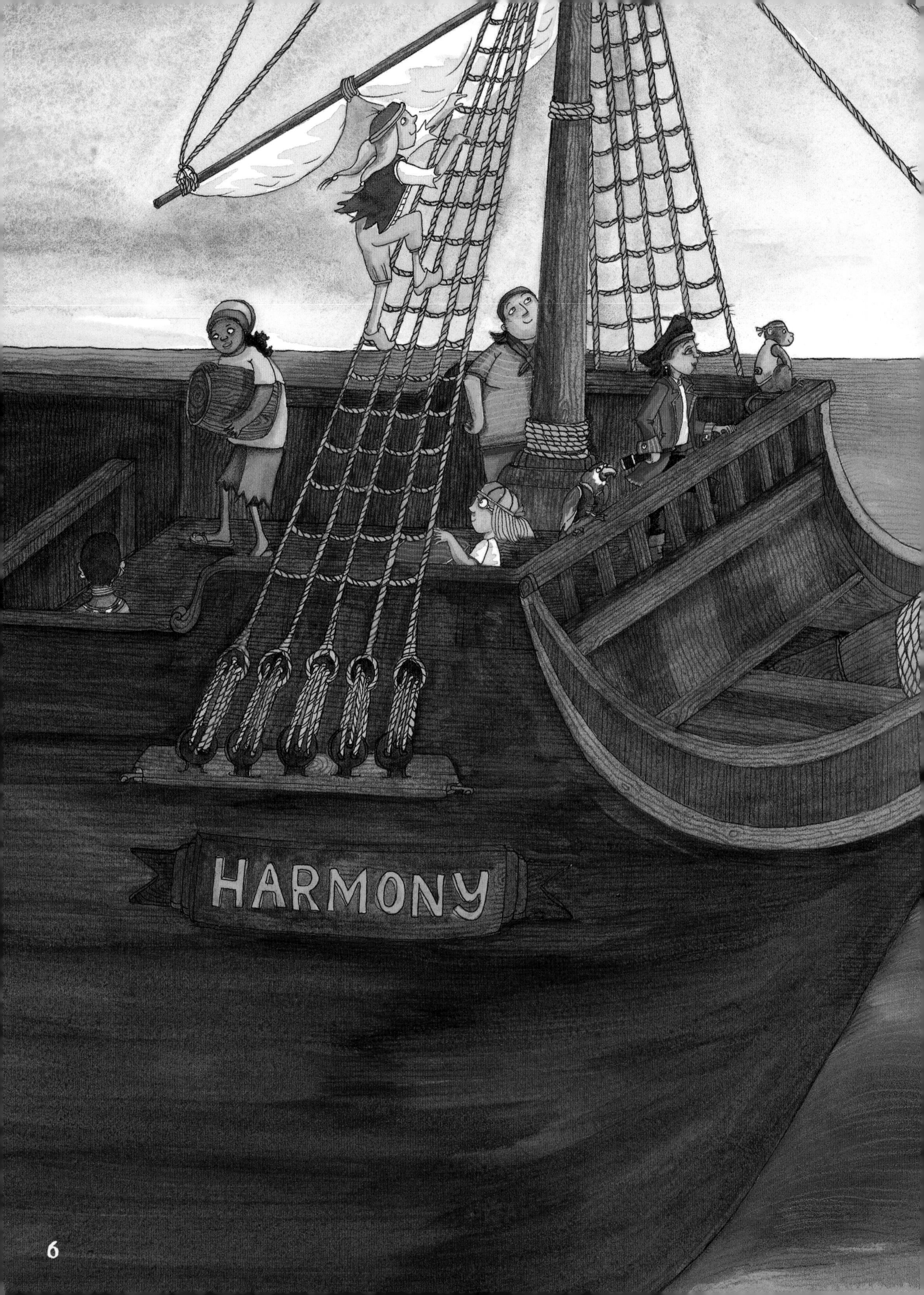
HARMONY

Pearl was the captain of her own ship — a large wooden vessel, solid and strong, that heaved and sighed as it rolled in and out of the foaming waves.

On warm sunny days, when the sea had gifted calm, Pearl would stand tall and proud at the bow of her sturdy ship. She would stare across the sparkling ocean knowing new and exciting adventures were just beyond the horizon.

Pearl had twenty-four crew on her ship — an interesting bunch indeed! These sailors had come from all parts of the world to join Captain Pearl Fairweather on the good ship *Harmony*.

Some women had ventured from China, and others from India and Pakistan. Some had travelled all the way from Russia, and many more from England and Africa. The sailors lived and worked together, and never a cross word was spoken.

Life was good on Captain Pearl's ship, and all was well… until one cloudy afternoon Captain Sandy McCross and his ship, the *Scurvy Dog*, came sailing by…

"Ahoy there! Ahoy there!"
shouted Captain McCross.
"Give me your ship! But I want
none of your useless crew!"

"Excuse me?" said Captain
Pearl Fairweather.
"Are you speaking to me?"

"Yes!" replied Captain McCross. "I am a pirate captain and I **want** your ship."

"Mmmm," answered Pearl, winking at her crew. "My ship is **not** for sale."

"I don't want to buy it, you silly goose!" shouted Captain McCross. "I'm going to **take** it for me own!"

Captain Pearl Fairweather did not answer.
She simply turned away from the rude
Captain McCross. Then, calmly and
with grace, she instructed her crew.
"Please turn our ship about," she said firmly.
"We will sail towards the Islands of Plenty,
and far away from the *Scurvy Dog*."

With this one instruction from their captain,
the crew went to work. The anchor was lifted
and the sails were hoisted. Ropes were tied
and the decks were cleared. The large brown
ship turned her massive hull about and sailed
away, leaving the *Scurvy Dog* and her motley
crew far behind.

13

The following day, as large storm clouds rolled in across the Islands of Plenty — so too did Captain Sandy McCross and the *Scurvy Dog*. And once more, the old wooden ship, with her dirty grey sails, pulled in alongside the good ship *Harmony*.

"Give me your ship!" shouted Captain McCross, yet again. "I want it for me own!"

With a twinkle in her eye, Captain Pearl replied, "Not on your nelly. This is **my** ship and **my** very fine crew. Never, ever speak to me in that rude manner again. Now, because I am a good and fair captain, I will offer you one piece of advice — if you want to survive this gathering storm, you will need to take shelter in the Bay of Tranquillity."

"Ha! Ha! Ha!" laughed the loud and rather silly Captain McCross. "A true pirate can weather **any** storm. The *Scurvy Dog* and her crew will stay right here!"

So once more, Captain Pearl Fairweather had her crew turn *Harmony* about and head for shelter, leaving the *Scurvy Dog* and her motley crew far behind.

Large clouds continued to roll in. They turned from grey to black to green. Lightning flashed and the sea grew large and fierce. *Harmony*, however, and her very fine crew were safely tucked away in the Bay of Tranquillity.

The *Scurvy Dog* and her crew were not so fortunate.
The old wooden boat tossed and rolled in the gigantic seas.

And as the sun came up, and the rain began to clear, all the crew including Captain McCross sat miserably in a small wooden lifeboat drifting towards the Bay of Tranquillity — their ship now a broken wreck on the ocean floor.

"Ahoy there! Ahoy there!" shouted Captain McCross as the small wooden boat drifted towards the large pirate ship.

Pearl, who was enjoying her early morning cup of tea, looked out to see a wet and bedraggled group of sailors floating in a small wooden lifeboat towards the stern of her ship.

"Mmmm," thought Pearl to herself, "the crew from the *Scurvy Dog*."

Pearl put her cup down and peered over the stern.

"I suppose you want my ship?" she asked of Captain McCross.

From his position far below the stern, Captain McCross
stared angrily up at Pearl.

"Put the ladder down," he demanded rudely.

"I want to come aboard."

"Mmmm," replied Pearl, deep in thought. "You may only board my ship if you agree to the following conditions:

1. That you all work with me and my crew in **peace** and **harmony**.

2. That you **never**, ever **think** you are better than anyone else on this ship.

3. That you show **respect** to all the sailors aboard this ship.

4. And that you **do not try to** take over my ship again!"

"Never!" replied Captain McCross. "I will **never** agree to these conditions."

Pearl looked towards the bedraggled sailors sitting in the old wooden lifeboat.

"And what of you?" she asked. "Will you agree to my fair and just conditions?"

One young lad with hair the colour of a rusty nail, cleared his throat with a little cough. He looked to Pearl and the other sailors as he spoke. "I will," he ventured. "I will be happy to abide by these conditions."

A rather old sailor with a long scraggly beard also spoke up.
"I will," he said.

"And I," said another.

"Me too," said the tall sailor with a red bandanna.

"And I," said another.

Before too long, all the sailors in the small wooden boat had agreed to Captain Pearl Fairweather's conditions.

All except one!

Captain Sandy McCross stood there, sour-faced and angry.

"I will **never** agree to your conditions," he shouted. "Never!"

"Then that is your choice," replied Captain Pearl Fairweather, and once again she turned away from his angry pout.

Before the sailors were allowed to board, a document was drawn up with all the conditions written out in full. One by one, each sailor boarded the ship and signed the document.

All except one.

As the last sailor boarded the ship and the rope ladder was rolled away, Captain Sandy McCross stood angrily in the small wooden boat.

Captain Pearl Fairweather instructed her crew, "Pull up the anchor and hoist the sails. We are sailing towards the horizon in search of adventure!"

The large ship moved peacefully away, leaving a small wooden boat all alone in a very large sea.

And from that day forward, the crew from the *Scurvy Dog* and the crew from the good ship *Harmony* worked together as one — sailing the ocean blue in search of adventure.

No-one really knows what happened to Captain
Sandy McCross. Although … some say he lived
out his days, lonely on a deserted island; while
others say he grew old and even grumpier
working as a kitchen hand on a transport ship.

But no-one **really** knows …